This book is dedicated to my children, Hayley and Ellie, who keep me on my toes, asking all sorts of questions that force me to continue to use my imagination. May these sweet girls never lose their infectious sense of curiosity.

www.mascotbooks.com

The Tooth Fairy's Tummy Ache

For more information, please contact:
Mascot Books
620 Herndon Parkway #320
Herndon, VA 20170
info@mascotbooks.com

Library of Congress Control Number: 2019904762

CPSIA Code: PRT0919A
ISBN-13: 978-1-64307-350-7

Printed in the United States

The Tooth Fairy's Tummy Ache

Lori Orlinsky

illustrated by Vanessa Alexandre

You see, it happened when I was eating
a juicy red apple for snack.

I was chewing and chomping when suddenly
I bit down and heard a crack!

My first tooth was finally out!
All it took was something yummy.

But when I went to collect it from my mouth,
I realized it had landed in my tummy!

This wasn't the plan
I had thought of in my head.

I had to think of something fast
before I went to bed!

I searched high and low
for something tiny and white.

Even though
what I was
doing wasn't
really right.

The Tooth Fairy
wouldn't visit
if she didn't have a
tooth to take.

So I put a kernel
of popcorn
under my
pillow
as a replacement
fake!

This child's tooth feels a little strange
and doesn't look quite right.

But I'll trade it for a silver dollar,
hop on my toothbrush, and fly out of sight!

Back to the workshop I go
to add this tooth to my collection.
But this one looks rotten
upon further inspection!

It's too round to string
and too tiny to glue.
What can I do with this tooth?
I don't have a clue!

I call my fairy friends
who come over skipping and hopping.
But when they get close to the tooth,
all of a sudden it starts popping!

Quickly it spreads
from the floor to the ceiling.

I know I should try to stop it,
but it's hunger that I'm feeling!

There's nothing left to do
but say "ahh" and open wide.

Popcorn rains in my mouth
and fills me up inside.

A few minutes later,
there isn't any mistaking.
I feel really yucky
because my tummy is aching!

So I stay in bed
and skip the work I need to do.
But what's going to happen
when everyone wakes up feeling blue?

The grandmas and grandpas
would be missing their new dentures.
My friends wouldn't have necklaces
for their dress up adventures!

The night sky would be without
all of its shiniest stars.
Tooth fairies wouldn't have flying dust,
so they'll have to drive cars!

Suddenly it hit me!
I had a hunch.
Maybe she lost this
  tooth
while she was
  having lunch!

I go through the window
for the second time tonight.

I had to explain to this girl
the difference between
wrong and right.

I tap on her shoulder
and whisper in her ear,
Lying won't get you anywhere.
Do you hear me, my dear?

It's best to be honest
and always tell the truth.
You should have just told me
that you swallowed your tooth!

She flashes me a smile
with a toothless grin.
And I feel a new friendship is
about to begin.

I'll leave you this notepad
so you can write me a letter.
When you lose your next tooth,
hopefully it'll work out much better!

Other books by Lori Orlinsky

Being Small
(Isn't So Bad After All)

Author photo by Jeff Bolek /
FlashBulb Photography

About the Author

Lori Orlinsky is a multi-award-winning children's book author based in Chicago. She is a lifetime member of the No Cavity Club, and her dentist always calls her a "superstar brusher." Inspired by her own experience misplacing her first tooth, Lori hopes this story will give kids a glimpse of what it is like inside the Tooth Fairy's workshop, as well as a lesson on honesty.